A

DIVE

into the

DEEP

by
Tessa Pfeifer

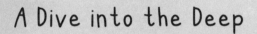

A Dive into the Deep

tessapfeifer.com

This book is dedicated
to my first storytellers.
Thanks, Mom and Dad.

Ophelia came home from school with a new library book.

She sat down to read on her chair by the window, her favorite reading nook.

The book was heavy and smelled like the sea.
What could be inside? Let's open it and see!

"Welcome!" A small voice cried out from the pages.
To explore the ocean you picked a good read!
Come with me,
follow my lead!

The wind blew hard as water
swirled around.

She whirled and twirled and felt her
toes leave the ground.

Welcome to the ocean,
there's so much to see!

There are **large** creatures and small
ones and every size in between!

There are so many animals that live down below.
Let's see who we can find before it's time to go.

Floating on waves like gentle
hills, pelicans keep fish
dinners safe in their bills.

Mammals like the dolphin come to the surface to breathe.

They fill up their lungs before diving beneath.

Some animals are flashy like the parrot fish.
Their scales shine like jewels as their
fins swirl and swish.

Some keep their treasures tucked out of sight...

Look very close, do you see a light?

The giant clam may have a plain looking shell,
but hidden inside a pearl may dwell.

The leafy sea dragon hides among the sea grass,
Keeping out of sight until danger has passed.

The humpback whale is too large to hide.

Swimming gracefully through the water
they dive and glide.

Some creatures don't have fins at all!

The octopus has eight arms
to swim and crawl.

Some fish live deep where
it's dark day and night.

The angler fish uses bioluminescence
to create its own light.

What other animals can
we meet today?

What's that ahead?
A spotted eagle ray!

These gentle giants glide through
the water with grace.

Watch out for their tail spine,
and give them plenty of space!

Some fish appear to soar through the sky.

The flying fish
dives, then leaps high high high!

We've had quite the adventure below,
but it's getting late and time to go.

Here we go, up up and away!

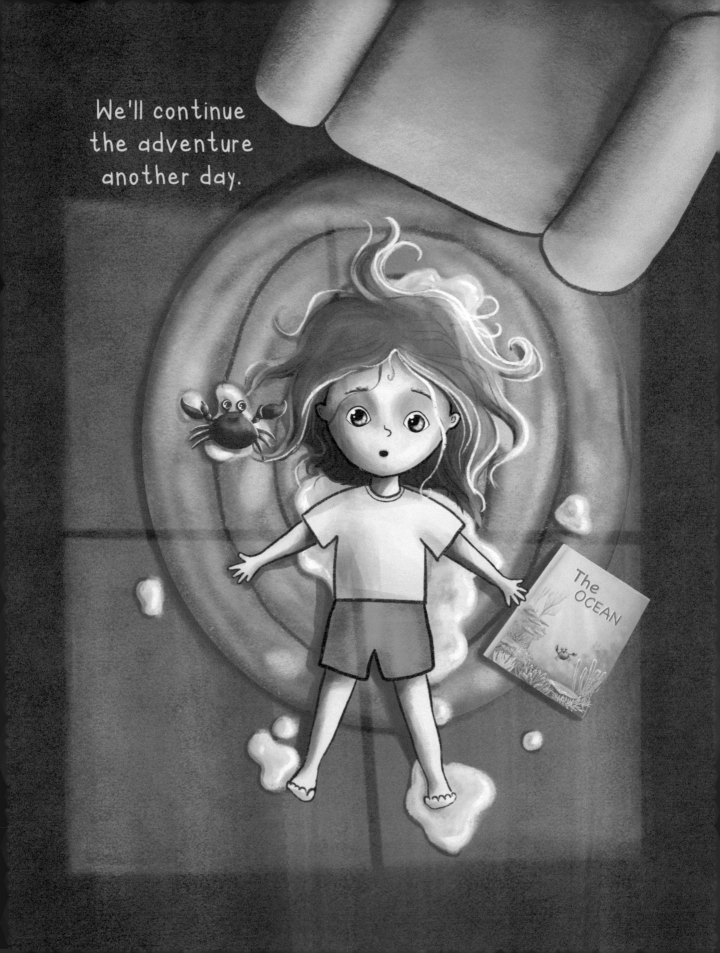

We'll continue the adventure another day.

Who knows where you'll go when you open a book...

...so crack it open and have a look!

About the Author

Tessa is an East Coast based artist with a background in marine science. She hopes her books inspire kids to look under rocks, love bugs, and explore the natural world around them.

Thank you!

Your voice means the world to me! If you enjoyed this book, please consider leaving a review on Amazon. Thank you for your support and for choosing this book, I appreciate you!